Cinderella

Adapted by Della Cohen

PaRragon

Bath · New York · Singapore · Hong Kong · Cologne · Delhi
Melbourne · Amsterdam · Johannesburg · Shenzhen

This edition published by Parragon in 2012
Parragon
Chartist House
15-17 Trim Street
Bath BA1 1HA, UK
www.parragon.com

ISBN 978-1-4075-6483-8
Printed in Poland

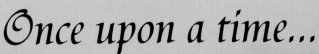

Once upon a time...

Long ago in a faraway land, poor Cinderella lived with her mean stepfamily. They filled her days with cooking, scrubbing, washing and chores of every kind.

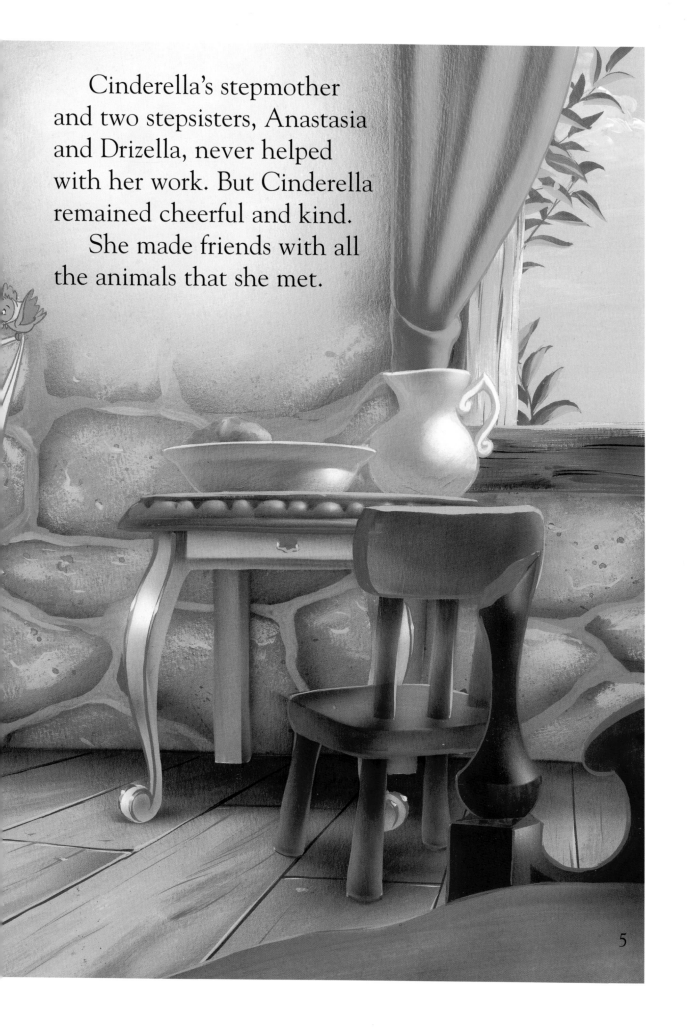

Cinderella's stepmother
and two stepsisters, Anastasia
and Drizella, never helped
with her work. But Cinderella
remained cheerful and kind.
She made friends with all
the animals that she met.

Cinderella even made clothes for the mice who shared her small attic room.

One day, Jaq, her favorite mouse, was upset.

"What's all the fuss about?" Cinderella asked.
Jaq led her to a new mouse, caught in a trap!

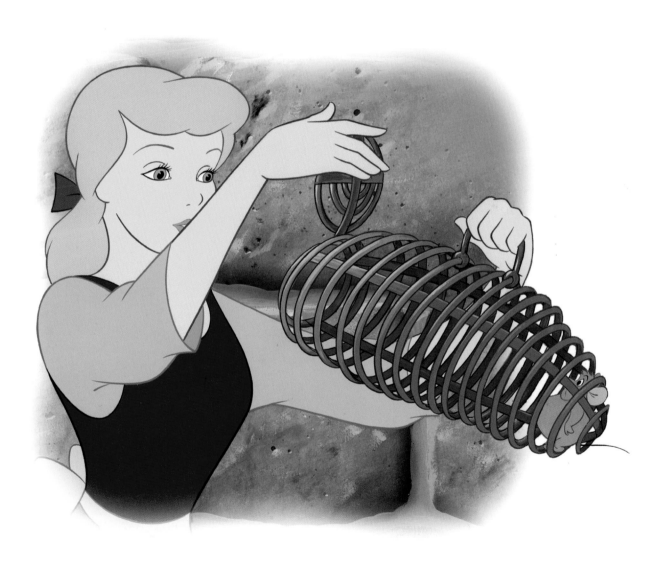

Cinderella quickly freed the frightened mouse.
Then she dressed him in new clothes and found
the perfect name for him: Gus.

When it was time for Cinderella to feed the chickens, the mice headed for the barnyard. Cinderella always saved some corn for them.

But today, the mean old cat, Lucifer, blocked their way. Jaq was chosen to get the cat to chase him. Then the other mice could scoot outside.

The plan worked. Jaq kicked the cat and angry Lucifer began chasing him.

But Jaq was too fast for Lucifer and made it safely into a mousehole. While Lucifer waited for Jaq to come out, the other mice scampered by him!

Cinderella spent the rest of her day attending to chores.

"Take that ironing," Drizella demanded.

"Don't forget the mending," Anastasia added.

"Pick up the laundry and get on with your duties," her stepmother ordered.

Meanwhile, at the royal palace, the King complained to the Grand Duke. "It's high time my son got married," he sobbed. "I want grandchildren!"

The King decided to hold a ball. "If all the eligible maidens come," said the King, "the Prince is bound to find his bride among them."

The Royal Ball

Later that day, Cinderella heard a knock on the door. "Open in the name of the King," said the royal messenger. He handed Cinderella an invitation.

When her stepmother read the invitation aloud, Drizella and Anastasia became excited. Each imagined the Prince falling in love with her.

Cinderella was also excited. "Why, that means I can go, too!" she said. The stepsisters laughed. "Every eligible maiden is supposed to attend," answered Cinderella.

Surprisingly, her stepmother agreed. "I don't see why you can't go . . . *if* you get all your work done, and *if* you can find something suitable to wear."

Cinderella raced to her room and found a dress that had belonged to her mother. With a little stitching, she could make it pretty.

As Cinderella worked on the dress, her stepmother and stepsisters called for her and gave her many chores. "Get them done quickly," said her stepmother.

When Cinderella had to put the dress aside, her animal friends began to work on it. They gathered beads and a sash that the stepsisters had thrown away.

Soon they had created a beautiful gown!

Cinderella finally finished her chores and
went to her room. Then she realized it was too
late to get ready for the ball. She was so sad!

Suddenly, the mice yelled, "Surprise!"

They showed Cinderella the beautiful gown.
"Oh, thank you so much!" she cried.

Cinderella put on the gown and hurried to join her stepfamily. But when her jealous stepsisters recognized their old sash and beads, they tore Cinderella's gown to shreds!

Cinderella's friends watched sadly as she wept in the garden. "It's no use," she sobbed. "Nothing will help."

At that moment, bright, sparkling lights began floating and swirling around Cinderella.

Poof! Cinderella's Fairy Godmother appeared. "Dry those tears," she told Cinderella. "You can't go to the ball looking like that."

"But I'm not going," said Cinderella.

"Of course you are," replied the Fairy Godmother.

She waved her magic wand over a pumpkin, and a regal coach appeared!

"Oh, it's beautiful," said Cinderella. The Fairy Godmother waved her wand again.

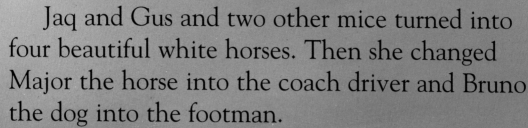

Jaq and Gus and two other mice turned into four beautiful white horses. Then she changed Major the horse into the coach driver and Bruno the dog into the footman.

Next, the Fairy Godmother turned Cinderella's torn dress into a beautiful gown. In a flash, there were also tiny glass slippers for her feet.

"On the stroke of midnight, the spell will be broken," the Fairy Godmother warned. "Everything will be as before."

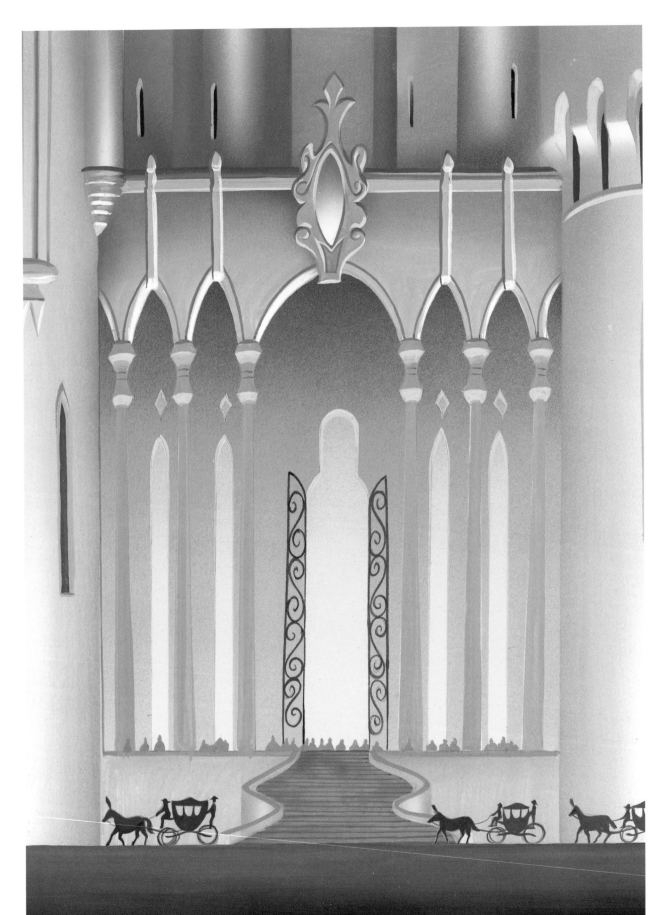

The Glass Slipper

The ball was just beginning when Cinderella arrived. She climbed the long staircase. *Oh, how happy I am*, she thought.

The King and the Grand Duke watched as the maidens walked forward to meet the Prince. The Prince was unimpressed with them all.

Then he noticed Cinderella.

Entranced, he walked past all of the other maidens and led Cinderella into the ballroom.

They began to dance.

They danced every
dance until . . . the clock
began to strike midnight.
Bong! Bong!

"I must go!" Cinderella cried in a panic, freeing her hand from the Prince's. As she fled, she lost a glass slipper on the staircase.

The clock sounded as the coach raced from the palace. It was midnight!

The horses were mice again.
Cinderella was in rags. But she
still had one glass slipper.

The next morning, the Prince proclaimed that he would marry the girl who had lost her slipper at the ball.

The Grand Duke would check every house in the kingdom for the maiden whose foot fitted the glass slipper.

Cinderella was so happy! She eagerly awaited the Grand Duke's visit.

No matter what Drizella and Anastasia ordered Cinderella to do, she nodded dreamily. Cinderella's stepfamily could not understand the reason for her joy.

Then, the wicked stepmother realized that it must have been Cinderella who was the Prince's favourite at the ball!

She locked Cinderella in her room.

"Let me out!" Cinderella cried.

But her stepmother put the key in her pocket, laughing her meanest laugh.

Then Cinderella heard a knock at the front door. The Grand Duke had arrived!

Meanwhile, Jaq and Gus had seen what the stepmother did. They took the key out of her pocket and slipped it under Cinderella's door.

Downstairs, the Grand Duke watched his footman try to squeeze Anastasia's big foot into the slipper. Of course, the slipper did not fit Drizella, either.

As she hurried down the steps, Cinderella heard the Grand Duke ask, "Are there any other maidens in the house?"

"Please wait!" called Cinderella. "May I try on the slipper?"

The angry stepmother tripped the footman as he approached Cinderella. The glass slipper shattered. "Oh, no!" moaned the Grand Duke.

"But you see," said Cinderella, reaching into her pocket, "I have the other slipper." Quickly, the Grand Duke put the slipper on Cinderella's foot.

It fitted perfectly! Cinderella was the Prince's love!

Cinderella married the Prince and lived happily ever after. And so did Jaq, Gus, and all of Cinderella's animal friends!